The Sun

by Colleen Sexton

Consultant:
Duane Quam, M.S. Physics
Chair, Minnesota State
Academic Science Standards
Writing Committee

BELLWETHER MEDIA · MINNEAPOLIS, MN

Note to Librarians, Teachers, and Parents:

Blastoff! Readers are carefully developed by literacy experts and combine standards-based content with developmentally appropriate text.

Level 1 provides the most support through repetition of high-frequency words, light text, predictable sentence patterns, and strong visual support.

Level 2 offers early readers a bit more challenge through varied simple sentences, increased text load, and less repetition of high-frequency words.

Level 3 advances early-fluent readers toward fluency through increased text and concept load, less reliance on visuals, longer sentences, and more literary language.

Level 4 builds reading stamina by providing more text per page, increased use of punctuation, greater variation in sentence patterns, and increasingly challenging vocabulary.

Level 5 encourages children to move from "learning to read" to "reading to learn" by providing even more text, varied writing styles, and less familiar topics.

Whichever book is right for your reader, Blastoff! Readers are the perfect books to build confidence and encourage a love of reading that will last a lifetime!

This edition first published in 2010 by Bellwether Media, Inc.

Library of Congress Cataloging-in-Publication Data

Sexton, Colleen A., 1967-
The sun / by Colleen Sexton.
    p. cm. – (Blastoff! readers. Exploring space)
Includes bibliographical references and index.
Summary: "Introductory text and full-color images explore the physical characteristics of the sun in space. Intended for students in kindergarten through third grade"–Provided by publisher.
ISBN 978-1-60014-400-4 (hardcover : alk. paper)
1. Sun–Juvenile literature. I. Title.
QB521.5.S46 2010
523.7–dc22   2009037984

Text copyright © 2010 by Bellwether Media, Inc.
Printed in the United States of America, North Mankato, MN.
010110   1149

Contents

The sun is a **star**. It is the center of the **solar system**.

The planets and all other objects in the solar system **orbit** the sun.

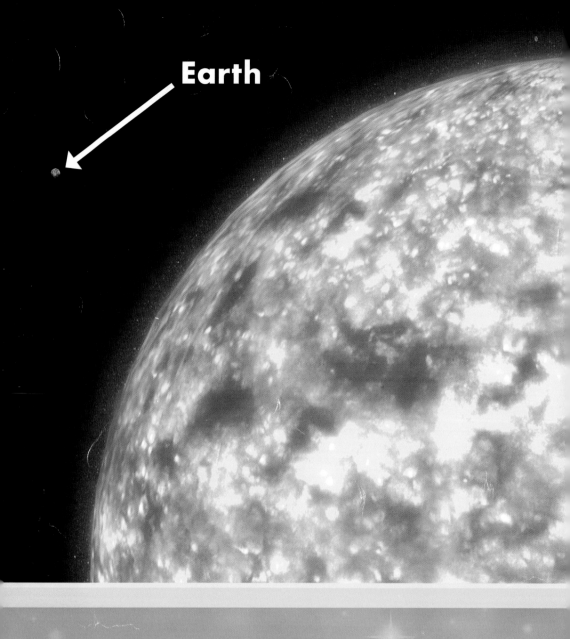

Earth

The sun is huge. More than one million Earths could fit inside the sun.

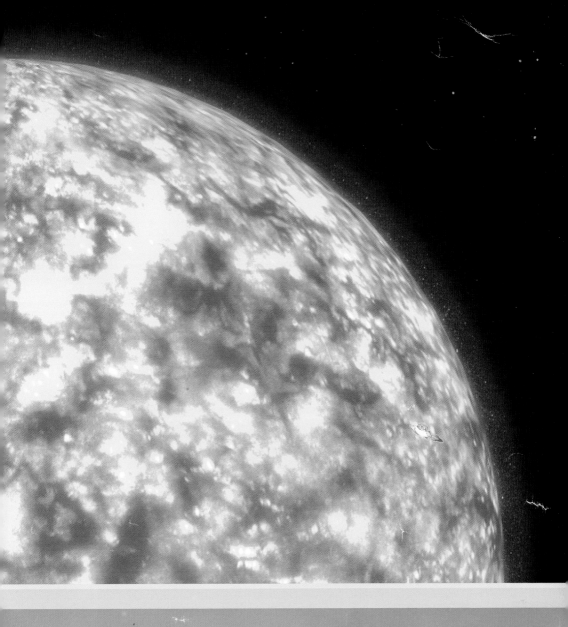

The sun is about 865,000 miles (1.5 million kilometers) wide. About 109 Earths could fit across the sun.

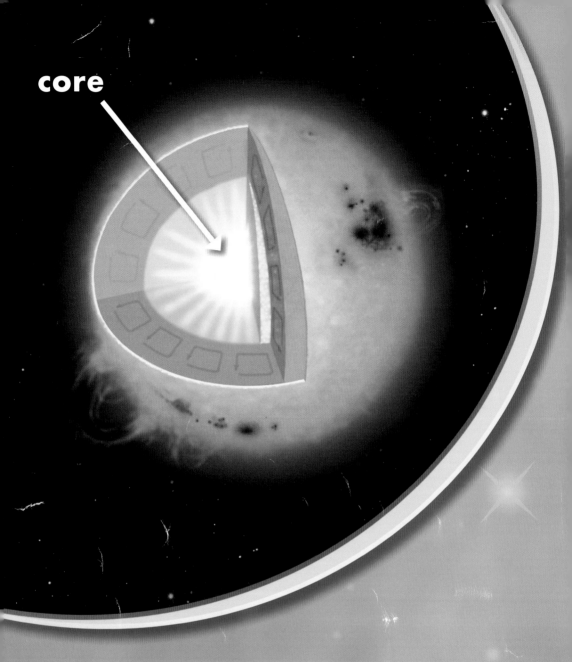

core

The sun is made of **gases**.
The gases smash into each other in
the **core** and let out **energy**.

The energy moves to the surface. It leaves the sun as light and heat. The light and heat reach Earth in only eight minutes!

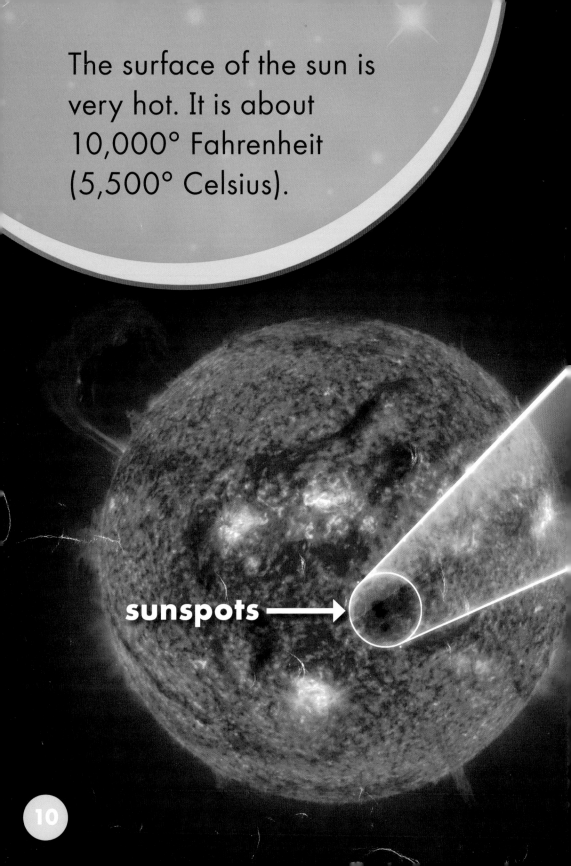

The surface of the sun is very hot. It is about 10,000° Fahrenheit (5,500° Celsius).

sunspots →

Sunspots appear on the sun. These dark patches are cooler than the rest of the surface.

The surface of
the sun bubbles.
Giant loops called
prominences
sometimes stretch
out from the surface.

prominence

solar flare

Explosions above the surface make **solar flares**. Gases from solar flares shoot out into space.

13

The sun sends out
solar wind. These streams
of gas flow through space.

Solar wind can make **auroras** in the night sky on Earth. Auroras are often bands of green, red, or purple light.

The sun is 93 million miles (150 million kilometers) from Earth. That is just the right distance. Earth is not too hot or too cold. People, animals, and plants can live there.

Earth

It takes Earth one
year to orbit the sun.
The seasons change as
Earth circles the sun.

17

day

night

Earth spins around once in a day.
From Earth, the sun appears to
move across the sky.

The sun's light only shines on half of Earth at a time. It is day where the sun shines. It is night where the sun does not shine.

The sun gives Earth heat and light. Its energy stirs Earth's **atmosphere** to make the weather. It gives us food by helping plants grow.

Without the sun, Earth would be a cold, dark place. The sun gives us the energy we need to live!

21

Glossary

atmosphere—the gases around an object in space

auroras—colorful lights in the night sky that appear when solar wind hits Earth; auroras can be seen most often in the far north and far south; they are also called northern lights and southern lights.

core—the center of the sun or a planet

energy—power that can be used; the sun's energy gives us the heat and light we need to live and work.

gases—matter that floats freely; the matter is close together at the core of the sun and it spreads out as it gets farther away from the core.

orbit—to travel around the sun or other object in space

prominences—giant loops of burning gases that shoot out from the sun's surface

solar flares—bursts of light and energy that explode from the surface of the sun

solar system—the sun and all the objects that orbit it; the solar system has planets, moons, comets, and asteroids.

solar wind—matter from the sun's gases that flows out into space

star—a large ball of burning gases in space; the sun is a star.

sunspots—dark patches on the surface of the sun that are cooler than the rest of the sun's surface

To Learn More

AT THE LIBRARY

Bredeson, Carmen. *What Do You Know About the Sun?* Berkeley Heights, N.J.: Enslow Publishers, 2008.

Howard, Fran. *The Sun.* Edina, Minn.: ABDO Publishing, 2008.

Landau, Elaine. *The Sun.* New York, N.Y.: Children's Press, 2008.

ON THE WEB

Learning more about the sun is as easy as 1, 2, 3.

1. Go to www.factsurfer.com.

2. Enter "the sun" into the search box.

3. Click the "Surf" button and you will see a list of related Web sites.

With factsurfer.com, finding more information is just a click away.

BLASTOFF! JIMMY CHALLENGE

Blastoff! Jimmy is hidden somewhere in this book. Can you find him? If you need help, you can find a hint at the bottom of page 24.

Index

Blastoff! Jimmy Challenge (from page 23).
Hint: Go to page 7 and put on your sunglasses.